"Ouch" was the first thing Chicken
Licken said. The second thing he
said was, "The sky is falling. I
must run and tell the King."

On the way across the farmyard,
he bumped into Henny Penny.
"Where are you going in such a
hurry?" asked Henny Penny as they
both picked themselves up.
"A piece of the sky has just
fallen on my head. I am going
to tell the King," said Chicken
Licken.

"I will go with you," said Henny Penny.

Cocky Locky was sitting on the
farmyard fence practising his crow.
"Where are you going in such a
hurry?" he asked in the middle
of a cock-a-doodle-do.
"We are going to tell the King
the sky is falling," said Chicken
Licken and Henny Penny, without
stopping.

"Then I will go
with you," said
Cocky Locky and
ran to catch up with them.

Ducky Lucky was swimming on the
pond.
"Where is everyone going in such
a hurry?" she asked.
"We are going to tell the King
the sky is falling," said Chicken
Licken, Henny Penny and Cocky Locky,
without stopping.

"Wait for me!" said Ducky Lucky.
"I will go with you." She
swam to the edge of the pond
and waddled after them.

Drakey Lakey was looking at
himself in a puddle.

"Why is everyone in such a hurry?"
he asked, as they splashed through
the puddle one after the other.

"The sky is falling. We must tell
the King," said Chicken Licken,
Henny Penny, Cocky Locky and Ducky
Lucky, without stopping.
"That sounds serious," said Drakey
Lakey, "I will go with you."

Goosey Loosey was looking for worms
in the mud.
"Where is everyone going in such
a hurry?" he asked.
"The sky is falling. We are on
our way to tell the King," said
Chicken Licken, Henny Penny, Cocky
Locky, Ducky Lucky and Drakey
Lakey, without stopping.

"I will go with you," said Goosey Loosey, spreading his great white wings. "I can look for worms later."

Turkey Lurkey was
scratching about
in the barn.
"Where are you
all going in such
a hurry?" he asked.
"To tell the King
the sky is falling,"
said Chicken Licken, Henny Penny,
Cocky Locky, Ducky Lucky, Drakey
Lakey and Goosey Loosey, without
stopping.

"Then I will go with you," said
Turkey Lurkey. "I have always
wanted to see the King."

Chicken Licken, Henny Penny, Cocky Locky, Ducky Lucky, Drakey Lakey, Goosey Loosey and Turkey Lurkey were hurrying along the footpath through the wood when they met Foxy Loxy.

"Where are you all going in such
a hurry?" asked Foxy Loxy.
"To tell the King the sky is
falling," they said, without
stopping.
"Then follow me," said Foxy Loxy,
"I know a short cut to the King's
palace."

But Foxy Loxy did not lead Chicken Licken, Henny Penny, Cocky Locky, Ducky Lucky, Drakey Lakey, Goosey Loosey and Turkey Lurkey to the palace. He led them to his own den where his family were waiting for him to bring them dinner.